Bridget
the Princess

Bridget the Princess

Written by
Abby Brough

Illustrated by
Badrus Soleh

XULON PRESS

Xulon Press
2301 Lucien Way #415
Maitland, FL 32751
407.339.4217
www.xulonpress.com

Paperback ISBN-13: 978-1-6628-3595-7
Hard Cover ISBN-13: 978-1-6628-3596-4

For My daughter Hannah

~A. B.

Bridget had waited through winter for
the first day of spring to appear.
This would be a great day to pretend
to be a princess!
She had gotten a dazzling tiara
for her last birthday and
today was the perfect day to wear it.

She raced down her stairs, out the door,
into the fresh spring air.

Birds flew by and
the grass was so green.

Only traces of snow remained and leaves were growing on the trees.

She twirled and twirled
around in her yard.

She picked the prettiest wildflowers she could find and gave them to her mama.

Today in the sunlight, her dazzling tiara sparkled. There were so many things she could find to do now that the sun was shining bright.

She soaked up the sun and
decided this had to be the best day ever!

But then...it began to rain.

Bridget didn't know what to do.
Tears filled her eyes. What is a princess
to do in the rain?

She couldn't pick flowers or twirl around the yard now. She sat and thought of some things that she *could* do, instead of the things that she *couldn't* do.

She *could* use her umbrella.
She *could* wear her tiara.
She *could* play in the rain.

Oh how happy she was to have her umbrella, wear her tiara, and play in the rain.

And that is just what she did!

The End!

CPSIA information can be obtained
at www.ICGtesting.com
Printed in the USA
LVHW071621040122
707840LV00002B/12